Mehrdad Shahmoradi Mofrad has an artistic background. He studied in Vienna's Art School and attended some semesters at the Vienna's Film Academy as a guest student and later as a part time student for a year.

Mehrdad Shahmoradi Mofrad

ENDLESS MISSION II

AUSTIN MACAULEY PUBLISHERS™
LONDON • CAMBRIDGE • NEW YORK • SHARJAH

Copyright © Mehrdad Shahmoradi Mofrad 2022

The right of Mehrdad Shahmoradi Mofrad to be identified as the author of this work has been asserted by the author in accordance with sections 77 and 78 of the Copyright, Designs and Patents Act 1988.

All rights reserved. No part of this publication may be reproduced, stored in a retrieval system, or transmitted in any form or by any means, electronic, mechanical, photocopying, recording, or otherwise, without the prior permission of the publishers.

Any person who commits any unauthorised act in relation to this publication may be liable to criminal prosecution and civil claims for damages.

This is a work of fiction. Names, characters, businesses, places, events, locales, and incidents are either the products of the author's imagination or used in a fictitious manner. Any resemblance to actual persons, living or dead, or actual events is purely coincidental.

A CIP catalogue record for this title is available from the British Library.

ISBN 9781398451292 (Paperback)
ISBN 9781398451308 (ePub e-book)

www.austinmacauley.com

First Published 2022
Austin Macauley Publishers Ltd®
1 Canada Square
Canary Wharf
London
E14 5AA

This is a fictional story, any similarities or resemblances to dead or living persons are purely coincidental and not intentional.

Characters

Major John Barr
General Paul Slyer
Major Simon Joyful
Dr Karen Balt
Andreas Benedict
Peggy Browning
Elisabeth Browning
Dr Karen Balt
A Child + A Woman
The Man=Johann Perch
Deborah Slyer
Train Conductor
Man 1
Man 2
Man 3

Scene 1
London, England
Somewhere in Kensington
A telephone booth
Rain is pouring down a telephone booth
A man is inside the telephone booth

Scene 2
Slyer's flat
Thunder and followed by lightning which enlightens the flat through the windows as the phone starts to ring.
Deborah picks up the telephone receiver.
She hears Man 1's voice and asks,

How did you know about me?

She hears Man 1 saying,
I'm not allowed to tell you that.
Do you still have any doubts?

Deborah
I can't say, I haven't!

Man 1
Why?

Deborah
You are playing a double game, aren't you?

Scene 3
Rain is pouring down, thunder and followed by lightning.

Man 1 continues,
Listen carefully, I don't want to prolong the war nor am...

Scene 4
Deborah's flat, she interrupts him and says,
That's why you made the gas, to shorten and to win the war?

Man 1
I'm not the one whom you are looking for, not a war follower...

Deborah
I didn't have that impression after following your invitation to the Chelsea house.

Man 1
Nevertheless, tell Slyer that we need to speak to him, after all, he is your husband and listens to you.
I'm willing to help.
Don't you think that he will need assistance from me, the enemy, who can also be an ally?

Deborah
I am not he, but I'll tell him your offer of collaboration.

Deborah puts the telephone receiver down and goes into the sitting room.

Scene 5
Sitting room

Slyer
You look pale, disturbing news?

Deborah
I want to get you to acquaint with some people.

Slyer
What for?

Deborah remains silent and smiles.

Slyer
Are you telling me something in secret?

Deborah
A sort of if you prefer, it concerns the gas, the Chlorine gas.

Slyer smiles.

Deborah
I knew you would like it.

Slyer
I wouldn't be sure if I were you.

Scene 6
Some days later.
Chelsea house.
In the sitting room a group of three men, General Slyer and Deborah Slyer are sitting around a table, mixed voices are audible, after a while, a distinctive voice of Man 1 is audible as he starts a conversation by saying,

The chemist will live and work in England.

Slyer
The chemist?

Deborah is silent. Slyer looks at him and asks,
Who are you and whom are you talking about?

Man 3
We are officials, diplomats if you would prefer.
We're talking about the person you are searching for.

Slyer
Whom am I searching for?

Man 1
"Chemist!" Wir brauchen Ihre Hilfe. (We need your help.)

Slyer
What does this chemist do?

Man 2, whilst the rest are silent, says,
Major Barr and Joyful must not find him.

Slyer
To find whom, who is this chemist?

Man 1
Ich bin nicht sicher, ob wir den Barr von weiteren Untersuchungen abhalten können.
(I am not sure if we could keep Barr from further investigations.)

Man 2
Samuel Judd's theatrical act became a ruthless and a bloody one.

Slyer interrupts him and says,
It hasn't passed you by unnoticed, has it?

Man 2 is becoming more responsive and says,
So, you know what we are talking about, do you not?

Slyer
I might, tell me more.

Man 2
If the chemist was present at this meeting, he would plead in favour of helping instead of being challenged.

Slyer
But he is not, or is he?

Man 2 realises that Slyer is intensifying the conversation by questioning, vehemently says,
Tell Barr that the man he is searching for is dead. He was assassinated in Germany.

Man 1
He might be dead by now.

Slyer looks at Deborah and asks,
Whom are these people talking about, Deborah?

Deborah
Paul, they want to keep "the Chemist", the one responsible for the Chlorine gas, here, in England.

Man 3
He might be contaminated by his chemical experiments by now.

Slyer pretends to be curiously interested, asks,
'The Chemist?' Will I ever become acquainted with this gentleman, "the Chemist"?

Man 3
In good time, you might, General.

Slyer
Is he here, with us, in this room?

Man 1
And if he were here, in this room, amongst us, what then?

Man 2 looks at Man 1 angrily and nods negatively.
Slyer looks at both of them and says,
I would try to convince him not to continue nor to develop further Gases and I would ask him to advise others to do the same. "Stop the productions!"

Man 2
Idealism has hardly ever changed the course of history or won any wars.

Slyer
Compromising might?

He looks at Deborah and continues saying,
That's why we are here, don't you agree?

Man 1
Just tell Barr, that the man is dead, and he must not continue the investigation and that is an order…yours of course!

Slyer looks at Deborah.
Deborah looks at him without saying anything.
Man 3 takes Slyer aside and continues,
You keep the secrecy of the chemist's living here!
He is not the devil, though the misuse of his chemicals, makes him become one.

Slyer
Even if I agree with you, it shall not justify its deadlines nor its consequences, as the Chemist most surely and intentionally with the purpose of quick mass murder, has produced it.

He looks at Deborah and remains silent.
Man 1 stares at Slyer and is seemingly not able to find more words as suddenly says,
Wenn (If), Ich(I)…If I could persuade you, General, to handle in yours and our mutual interests?

Slyer
I hardly find some, do you think, there are any?

Man 1
Suchen Sie danach und Sie werden welche finden. (Search for some and you shall find.)

Slyer says the following with a lower voice,
Tell me Deborah, is 'the Chemist' amongst us?

Deborah
I don't know him, I can't tell.

Slyer
Who are these people?

Deborah
They are our German counterparts.

Slyer
Counterparts in times like these!

Man 2
Beruhigt Ihr euch und überlegt Ihr euch unsere Vorschläge. (Calm yourselves and take our suggestion into consideration.)

Deborah and Slyer look at one another, stand up, and leave the room, the rest remain silent and sitting.

Scene 7
Hospital
Ward 1
John is lying on a bed and is looking at the woman who is sitting next to his bed. She is reading from a medical board. She finishes her reading and looks at John.

John
Is it the end?

Balt is listening and looking at him silently.

John
End of this mission?

Balt
You are recovering from your shot wound.

John
What about the others?
James Browning, is he also, here in this ward?

Balt
James Browning is dead.

John
Dead?

Balt
Two other persons, a woman, and a man are also dead.

John's voice begins to get lower as he asks,
Am I beyond the mission's end?

He raises his voice and asks,
Is it safe here?

Balt is looking at him, answers,
Yes, it is safe here.

John [whispers]:
The monotonous and bold attempts of finding the scientist behind the mass-murderous chlorine gas turned into a mephitic mission…

Balt is still looking at him and does not involve in his whispering, says,
you have visitors.

John
Visitors?
Peggy and Elisabeth Browning come into the room and come nearer to John's bed.

Balt tells the visitors,
He is still weak and needs rest, keep your visit as short as possible.

Balt leaves the room. John looks at both of them as they are sitting down and shortly afterwards, he says,
James Browning, a good friend, and good colleague…

Peggy
A good brother.

Elisabeth
And a loving husband.

John
Unfortunately, I couldn't prevent it. It all happened so suddenly and so briskly…
I guess we are getting used to being over-rolled…
…You excuse me, I am…

He closes his eyes.
Peggy and Elisabeth leave the room.

Scene 8
At Balt's Ordination, in the hospital, Balt is sitting behind her desk facing General Slyer who is sitting opposite her, and says,

Balt
He mentioned a 'Mission'.

General who is waiting for her to continue, asks,
And…Did he mention any details?

Balt
No, no details.

General
I will have to question him.

Scene 9
Some days afterwards, a sunny day in a garden outside of ward 1,
John, Balt, and General are sitting around a table.

General starts a conversation,
Major John, it is nice to see you recover.

John looks at him without answering.

General
Tell me what happened. Why so many shots?
She could have taken it alive and help us find out more about their activities here.

John
It happened…

He feels uncomfortable, turns to a side whilst still sitting, and continues,
How, I don't know, I even let go of the trigger…

Slyer
German mission, tell me about German mission, in front of her?

Slyer
Yes, she is discreet.

John
In the German mission, we could put a group of assistants who were working in the laboratory under our control. One of them by the name of 'Hans Benedict', led us to a Liverpool address which we went to…

He drinks his tea and continues saying,

…to see his cousin, Andreas Benedict. Whilst we were observing Benedict's house in Liverpool, two persons went into the house.

General
Could you identify them?

John
No.

General
Do you think that Hans Benedict misled you and Browning in Germany?

John
Considering what happened after we returned from Germany, yes…Can we continue tomorrow? I feel tired.

Balt nods positively *whilst looking at the general.*

General
Yes.

Scene 10
Ward 1
Night of the same day
John gets out of his bed, changes his clothes, and goes out of the ward.

Scene 11
He goes through the corridor to the hospital's kitchen.

Scene 12
He reaches the kitchen and goes in.

Scene 13
He uses the kitchen's rear exit door and walks out of the hospital.

Scene 14
Outside of the Hospital
He walks to the railway station in the vicinity of the hospital. Its main entrance door becomes visible as he approaches it.

Scene 15
The next day in Balt's Office, she is speaking on the telephone saying,
He flew out of the hospital late last night.

Scene 16
General Slyer's Office.

Major Joyful is sitting opposite Slyer, on the other side of General's desk, and is also listening to the general's conversation as he says,
I didn't see any reasons for posting a guard in front of his room.

Scene 17
Balt's Office

Balt
Yes, it wasn't foreseeable.

Scene 18
General's office
Let me know as soon as he comes back.
He finishes the conversation on the phone, puts the receiver on the hook, looks at major Joyful, and asks Joyful,
Is the report on Barr's revolver?

Joyful
Sir, the examination of his revolver determines that the revolver's barrel malfunctioned.

General
You will be on your way.

Joyful
Sir.

Scene 19

John is sitting in a train compartment with a couple and a child. The child is staring at John who is looking through the window to the landscape, which is floating away in front of him. His attention is drowned, without turning his head, he hears the child's mother saying,
You should not stare at people.

She looks at John and says,
I apologise.

John
Not at all.

She continues,
We are going to Liverpool. Are you visiting Liverpool too or do you live there?

John turns his head to the child and smiles, the child smiles back at him.

John
I shall be visiting a friend,

Whilst he is still wearing the smile on his face and looking at the child. He turns his head back and continues looking through the window. The man looks at the woman and they both look at John.

Scene 20

Liverpool's Train Station. The train arrives, stops and John steps out of the train.

Scene 21

The main gate of the railway station. He comes out of the station, goes to the taxi station, and gets into a taxi. The taxi drives away from the railway station.

Scene 22

John is looking through the window.
He is looking at the pedestrians and cars which are passing the taxi.
The taxi reaches the address which John gave the taxi driver.

Scene 23

He gets out of the taxi and goes to the bench, at a distance, opposite the house in which Andreas Benedict lives, he sits on the bench.
After some time, a car arrives at the same address, halts, the couple and the child, from the train, get out of it and walk toward the house.
The man knocks on the door, Andreas opens, greets them and they go inside the house.

Scene 24

Inside the house
In the sitting room
The couple and Andreas are sitting around a table and the child is playing with a small toy train.
A conversation begins,

Andreas
What does he want here?

The woman
I had a short conversation with him on the train.

Andreas
And?

The Man
He will ring your bell.

Andreas
He looks at the man, the child, and says,
Yes, I suppose he would. I will have to go back to Germany.

The woman
She looks at him, takes the child's hand, and leaves the room with the child.

Andreas
Looks at the man and says,
Did you have to bring them along?

The Man
She insisted on coming along.

Andreas
I must take them back with me.

The Man
She misses your cousin, her husband.

Andreas
You know that it is a false cousinhood.

The Man
She doesn't know.

Andreas
That is not an urgent matter. I can tell her the truth on our way back to Germany.
You stay here and deal with the British agents.

The Man
He puts his hand into his jacket and takes a pistol out of his shoulder holster, checks the munition's magazine, replaces it with the one which he takes out of another jacket's pocket, puts it back in his holster, and puts the first magazine in his jacket's pocket.
Andreas who has been watching him, says and asks:
Johann Perch, you don't look well.
Why are you fiddling with that pistol?
Stop it, a shot might go off!

Perch
Sooner or later, it must.
You must leave now, use the backdoor.

Andreas gets out of the room and goes into the room where the woman and the child went into.

Scene 25
Meanwhile outside the house
The bench which John was sitting on, is unoccupied as he is walking away from it.

Scene 26
Outside the house
John goes toward the house.
He reaches the front door, waits for some seconds, and rings the bell.
There isn't an answer to the bell's ringing, he presses the bell's button once again, suddenly the doors open, and he faces a pistol, which is in front of his face.

Scene 27
Inside the house

Perch
Did you follow us?

John is silently looking at him and smiles.

Perch
Oh, I see you are in a good mood. Is it a friendly visit?

John
It depends:

Whilst keeping his smile and stops smiling as Perch asks:
Tell me why you are here if it is not a secret.

John answers calmly:
I don't have any secrets.

Perch is playing with the pistol in his hand.

Perch
Are you armed?

John
No, I am not, I mean no harm.

Perch puts down the pistol on the table next to him and asks:
What's your name?

John
My name is Barr, John Barr.

Perch
Good day John Barr, my name is Johann Perch. Since you are here, anything to drink?

John
No, thank you.

Perch
How can I help you: you need something from me, otherwise you wouldn't have been here?

John
Yes, you might Mr Perch. You might be able to help me to understand and with your help, even be able to find someone.

Perch
Whom?

John
Where is Mr Andreas Benedict who lives in this house, and of course the woman and the child?

Perch
Let's forget them for a moment and talk about you and me.

John remains silent as Perch continues:

Perch
Think about how you can save your life and your future which can be more prosperous and healthier than the one you might be experiencing.

John pretends to be becoming persuaded by Perch's suggestions for a possible cooperation with him responds:
It depends on…

Perch
No, it doesn't depend on anything…Only on trusting one another!

John
What do you want to entrust me with?

Perch
With secrets. Remember life is only a breath.

John

Indeed, but one particular breath is poisoning another man's breath.

Perch

Which one of them is to be saved? The poisoner or the poisoned one?

John

Both. May I stand up? My legs need movement.

Perch nods positively.
John stands up and starts to move around…

Perch

As you see, there hasn't been a stop to the production of chemical gases and they're spreading out to other countries.
They're being used as we speak right now.
We have to live with it and its secrets.

John

Live with it?

He is walking in front of Perch.

You can reveal its secrets.

Perch who is watching him walking asks:
What are you really looking for?

John doesn't answer and continues walking.

Perch
You find me only here:

Whilst putting the pistol in his left hand and with his right hand, he takes a packet of cigarettes out of his jacket's pocket, takes one cigarette out of it, lights it on, puts the pistol back in his right hand,
John is watching Perch's movements whilst Perch is still sitting as Perch suddenly says:
Secrets? You know everything.

John
You look pale, aren't you feeling well? Telling secrets lightens your burden.

Perch
Never mind how I seem to look.
I tell you one secret: 'As soon as the war is over, the gas will no longer be used.'

John
I like to listen to you telling me more of these sorts of secrets
Now I tell you one secret: 'Conventional weapons which are used in the wars, have also been used after the wars.'

Perch
That's not a secret. Do you think that there would be an 'Afterward'…after this war, I mean?

He turns slightly with his back to John to take a glass of wine, on the table behind him, as John who has been getting closer

to the table where the bottle is, suddenly jumps on Perch's right hand which holds the pistol, grabs it, holds Perch at the point of it and says:
Yes, I think so, there will be an "Afterward".

Perch who does not seem to be surprised, says:
Now what? Do you want to shoot and kill me?

John
I might.

Perch
One more secret: 'The pistol is empty.'

John points the pistols to the carpeted floor, pulls the trigger to fire a shot, realises that the pistol is, indeed empty.
He remains silent for a short while and says:
You are very sure of yourself, aren't you? Is there a reason for it?

Perch
Yes, I am…I intended to help.

John
Do you seriously intend to?

Perch
You and your other colleagues have been looking for the scientist behind the Chlorine GAS, haven't you?

John remains silent and is still looking at Perch.

Perch

No?

…Awaiting an answer…

John

Will you tell me now where Andreas Benedict might be?

Perch

What a difference can that make now?
John remains calm and says:
I do not know, tell me.

Perch

I know the man you people are after. It might even be a woman, a female scientist!
I mean, I know the scientist, 'the Chlorine Gas Chemist'.

John

That's interesting: 'the Chemist'.
Would you mind telling me who he or she is?

Perch

No, not at all. I might even take you to him.

John is still calm, whilst Perch who has been sitting, stands up and comes closer to John, looks into John's eyes, and says:
Suppose: He was standing in front of you, just like now as I am standing in front of you, what would you do to him?

John
No harm, that I assure you.

Perch
Would you believe me, if I was, he, the Chemist, I mean?

John is silently looking at him as Perch continues:
I am he, believe me, I am he!

His eyes are wide open,
John is still looking at him and smiles.
Perch starts to move around whilst saying:
Would this satisfy you?

John who is listening and looking at him begins to walk with him around the room and starts the conversation anew by asking him:
What are you?

Perch stops and says:
The path of destruction.

John
What do you mean?
Why are you here, so bitter and full of hatred?
Were you engaged in the development of the Gas?

Perch
So many questions, though not the one you're looking for, to be answered.

I can tell you that I was involved in the suffering part of it, to start with.

John
Suffering part of it, in what form?

Perch
You are witnessing my suffering with your eyes…
…But it is not why I am here.

John grabs Perch on his jacket and asks:
Answer me: what are you here for?

Perch
I do not know, maybe you can help me with an answer.

He seems to be sinking deeper into John's arms whilst John is holding him,

John
Come with me to our headquarters in London.

Perch *looks at him and says:*
I am contaminated by my deadly invention.

John
You are suffering, either by the state of mind or physically? Or both?

Perch
Yes, probably both and for quite some time.

John

Maybe we find out why, after the medical examinations in our headquarters.

Perch

You know as well as I do that there isn't a cure for it, not at present and probably not in the future.

John

We shall know more in London.

Perch

Now you are starting to believe that I am the one who produced the gas.

John looks at him and says:
I am looking at a sick man who needs care and attention and might be hallucinating.

Scene 28
In a train
John and Perch are sitting in a train compartment.
Perch opens a conversation by asking:
Do you think you are doing the right thing?

John remains silent.

Perch
Taking me to your headquarters, I mean.

Why can't we settle this: 'Whatever you might call it': between us here and now?
Have you not enough authorities?

John
You haven't provided me with any evidence to support you of being the scientist behind the Chlorine Gas. You even claimed him to be she, a female scientist!

Perch
Well, yes, but 'the Chemist', not to forget that he is a HE: 'the Chemist': a male chemist.
I am telling you: I'm him!
John is silently listening,

Perch
I don't need any proof for becoming what I have become.

John
Do you want us to acknowledge your chemical achievements and offer you a safe place?

Perch stands up and grabs John on John's jacket.
John manages to push him back and holds Perch to the wall of the compartment, keeps his right hand on Perch's throat, and sets to strangle him.
Perch with a low voice:
Take your hands off me.

John says with a loud voice:
Breathe!

whilst he is keeping his right-hand tide on Perch's throat. At the same time, the train slows down and stops.

Scene 29
Outside John's compartment on the train's corridor:
The train conductor is walking through the corridor as he reaches their compartment, he hears a loud cry saying:

John
Breathe, I say!

the *conductor stops, knocks on the door, and asks:*
Is everything alright in there, sir?

Scene 30
Perch with a very low voice:
I can't…

John loosens his hands on Perch's throat and with loud voice answers:
Yes, everything's fine, my friend is hard of hearing.

Scene 31
On the corridor, the conductor says:
Alright, sir.

As he walks away from the door, another passenger is passing him by, asks him where the lavatory is, and with his right-hand takes the conductor's general key which is hanging from his belt without him noticing it.

Scene 32

Inside the compartment
John takes his hands away from Perch's throat and says:
It would have been easier to use the Chlorine Gas.
Wouldn't you agree?

Perch who is getting calmer and is breathing regularly again looks at him and answers:
Yes, it would have been easier for you and dreadful for me to die of it…

John pushes him and drops him on the compartment seat, turns his back to him, looks to the wall on which he had held Perch before, and says:
Is it not what you are looking for? To breathe death?
Do you want others to follow you and to do the same?

He turns to Perch and asks:
Isn't it?

Perch who is sitting looks at him in silence.
He seems to be lamed and to be sinking deeper until almost laying on the seat on which he is sitting.
John sits next to him, lays his head back, and closes his eyes.
After some minutes of silence, the door to their compartment opens and Andreas bursts into the compartment.
John who is still sitting tries to stand up but he is pushed back by Andreas as he points a pistol at John's face and John remains sitting.

Perch

Was machst du hier Andreas? Wo ist sie, und das Kind, wo sind sie?
(What are you doing here Andreas? Where is she and the child, where are they?)

Andreas

Sie nahmen den früheren Zug.
Ich bin hier, um dich zu retten.
(They took the earlier train. I am here to save you.)

Perch

Ich kann nicht mehr gerettet werden.
(I can no longer be saved.)

Andreas

Du meinst, dass du nicht nach Deutschland zurück willst? Aber du bist noch wertvoll für uns.
(Do you mean that you do not want to come back to Germany? But you are still valuable to us.)

John Looks at Andreas and asks him in, German:
Ist er der Mann, den er behauptet zu sein? Der Chemist der das Chlor Gas produziert hat?
(Is he the man he claims to be?
The chemist who produced the Chlorine Gas?)

Andreas takes a look at Perch and answers John:
You don't really want me to trust you with an answer, do you, John Barr?

Perch
It is over, Andreas.

Andreas
We will bring it under control again. Trust me just one more time.

John is listening to the conversation between the two and interrupts by saying:
He has a different attitude now that he has had an encounter with the truth.

Andreas
What truth?

Whilst he is still pointing his pistol at John.
Johann with a lower voice says:
Put the pistol away!

John
How about you, Andreas, are you also facing the deadly truth of the Gas?

Andreas
I don't know…I don't care.

John
But you care about him.

Andreas
Of course, I care about him but…

I don't know, just leave me in peace.
By the way: how about you: John Barr, aren't you feeling a self-condemnation for all of that happened to your comrades?

John remains silent and looks at Johann Perch.
Andreas looks at Perch.

Perch
Time is running out. We must start anew to find a way out.

Andreas
A way out?

Perch
You said: 'Trust me just one more time.'

Andreas
Yes, I know what I said, but…

He doesn't seem to find words to continue with…

Perch
There aren't any more options open.

He looks at John and continues:
You must find Fred…

Andreas shouts at Laud and interrupts him by saying:
Say no more…

John
Fred…How can I find this Fred…? Is he perhaps called: 'Frederich?'

Perch and Andreas look at one another and afterwards Perch looks at John without answering him.
John who realises that he will not get an answer continues:
Speak up the name!

Johann
Fred…Hub…

Andreas shouts,
Johann!

John
Fred…Hub?

Andreas
No, stop Johann!

John
Why?

Andreas
Do you think you can force him into revealing the name?

John
Why not?

Andreas looks at Perch and sees that Perch is desperate and seemingly ill, asks him helplessly:
Johann sag etwas, lass mich nicht hier allein stehen!
(Johann say something, don't let me stand here alone.)

Andreas is turning slowly his head around and makes a weary impression…
…John notices that Andreas is intending to unlock his pistol and getting ready to shoot him with his fingers.
At that moment as Andreas is not looking at John but is still pointing the pistol at John, John jumps on Andreas, tries to get the pistol out of Andreas' hand by turning it to the left and the right as a shot is accidentally fired.
John and Andreas look at one another to see which one of them is shot at.
Andreas turns his head to Perch, sees that Perch is deadly shot in the left eye,
At this moment John knocks Andreas with a punch in Andreas' belly.
He falls and John fastens Andreas' hands from behind with the towel which was hanging by the washbasin and throws him on the floor.
John sits down and looks around him, closes his eyes and after a while, the door to the compartment opens and Major Joyful walks in with two soldiers who remain standing by the door behind him.

Major Joyful
Major Barr, John Barr?

John
What, who?

Joyful
I am Major Joyful. I have been instructed by General Slyer to look for you.

John asks with a lower voice:
… 'Joyful?' Look for me?

Major Joyful who does not hear properly what John is saying, answers:
Actually, look for and after you.

John *looks around him, to the dead Perch, to Andreas who is sitting on the compartment's floor, and to the soldiers behind Major Joyful.*
He breathes deeply in and out, stands up, and asks suspiciously:
Looking for or after me?

Joyful remains silent at the same time the train starts to move and gains speed.

Scene 33
London
Foreign Intelligence Office
General Slyer's Office
General Slyer is looking at John and looks at the file in front of him on the table:

Major Barr, you have not been fully successful in identifying Perch and uncover his activities in this case.

John

No, sir. He couldn't verify to be the scientist behind the Chlorine Gas, furthermore, he insisted that it is not a scientist but a chemist whom we are looking for.

But he almost pronounced some name by abbreviations of: "Fred…Hub…"

General

'Fred Hub', and further?

John

Nothing further, sir. That is all we know at present.

Slyer

How about the: 'Andreas Benedict'?

John

Benedict?

General

You seem to need assistance.
Major Joyful will assist you.

John

'Joyful', sir?

General
Yes, Major Joyful, Major Simon Joyful.

John
Yes, sir.

General closes the file in front of him and hands it over to John.
John stands up and leaves the office.

Scene 34
Hyde Park
Peggy and Elisabeth Browning are sitting on a Park bench.
Elisabeth starts a conversation:
It happened by that tree there.

She raises her hand and with her forefinger points to the tree where commander Judd was murdered and continues:
James told me commander Judd was murdered in front of that tree.

Peggy
How awful.

Elisabeth
Yes, a murderous business it is…But look there, I think I have seen that man before.

Peggy
Whom?

Elisabeth

The man who is going to that bench.

Peggy turns her head to have a look in that direction.

Elisabeth

Let us go for a short walk and have a chat with him.

They stand up.

Scene 35

General Slyer sits next to Man 3, takes a newspaper out of his mantle pocket, and holds it in front of himself.

Man3 starts a conversation whilst he is reading the newspaper says:

Have you thought about your interests?

Major Barr must be kept away from the case.

Slyer

I can't take the case away from him without proper reasoning.

Man 3

What do you require?

Slyer

If I am allowed to meet 'the Chemist', I will probably understand the situation better.

I might find reasons to convince myself and the others involved to keep away from the chemist.

Man 3 turns a page and says,

I am afraid that is not possible since none of our group has met him and most definitely never will.

John holds the newspaper lower, looks around, and says,
You do not let any options open to me.

Man 3
Convince Major Barr that the production of the Chlorine Gas is no longer an exclusive one and hasn't anything more to do with the chemist.

Slyer
Finding the chemist and holding him accountable, has become his obsession.

He holds the newspaper higher in front of his face.

Man 3
Now you realise the situation which we are in.

John speaks with a very low voice as he says,
There must be a compromising solution.

Man 3
Did you say anything?

John
Yes, any alternatives?

Man 3

You will have to find an explanation for your officers, or we must liquidate him and major Joyful, both of them, do you understand?

He stands up and leaves Slyer.
Slyer remains sitting, after a while, he says with a lower voice.
Am I corrupt enough to be a deceiver?
…Will I ever be able to pull myself out of this devilish plot that has been forming itself so rapidly?
I must find a way to stop it.

He closes his eyes and leans back on the bench.
Now Peggy and Elisabeth are standing in front of Slyer and we hear only their voices throughout, Slyer's eyes are still closed.

Peggy (Voice)

Can you hear me, sir?
Slyer opens his eyes and answers.
What? Oh, yes of course.

Elisabeth (Voice)

We saw a man who was sitting next to you and as he left you, you seemed to be becoming unconscious.

Peggy (Voice)

Aren't you feeling well General Slyer? You are General Slyer, aren't you?

Slyer
No, Yes, I am Sly…
…slightly under the weather…!

Peggy (Voice)
I am Peggy Browning, and this is my brother's widow, Elisabeth Browning.

Slyer
Browning you say?
I am so sorry about what happened to him, very awful, indeed.

Elisabeth (Voice)
Have you found out more about my husband's murder case?

Slyer says.
No, I am afraid nothing concrete yet.
This case is still under investigation.
I beg your pardon, but I have to go now…

Slyer *stands up and goes.*

Scene 36
The next day
Thames Promenade
John reaches the bench where James and he used to sit on and sits down.
He is watching the people who are passing by in front of him.
After a short time, he hears some steps as they approach him from behind the bench, he doesn't move nor turns to see who it is.

Now the steps have stopped, and he speaks.
Joyful, it is you.

Joyful
How did you know?

John
I had a guess. Do you want to speak to me?

Joyful
Yes.

John
Do come and sit.

Joyful sits next to him and speaks.
I know from your previous reports that major Browning and you used to sit on this very bench.

John
Yes, reports must be always thorough.

Joyful
Major Barr…

John interrupts him and speaks.
You may call me 'John'.
And may I call you 'Simon'?

Joyful
Yes…

The last time he and you sat here, was it the day before both of you went to Liverpool, is that correct?

John
Yes, that is correct…

After a short pause, John says,
We were so deeply involved in our investigations that the idea of 'Giving Up', didn't occur to us.

Joyful
How do you want to proceed now? A trip to Liverpool, perhaps?

John
No, I am afraid we will not find anyone there any longer… They have left Liverpool by now.

Joyful
But we still have 'Hans Benedict' in Germany.

John
'Perch', puzzled me by an irritating game.

Joyful
What would we gain in finding 'the Scientist' or as Perch put it 'the Chemist' behind the Chlorine Gas now that it is everybody's choice of a weapon of mass murder?

John
I do not know, perhaps we find out the real reasons for its production, if it was accidental and why it was given for military use?
Furthermore, whether or not there would be more deadly chemical weapons that are about to be produced based originally on it.

Joyful realises how important this mission for John has become and asks,
Do you not feel a personal obsession, revenge for what has been happening to you and your colleagues in this case?

John looks at Joyful for a short while and says,
All the intelligence work, sacrifices, and lost lives must not remain unrewarded.
Some people must be held responsible for the poisonous chlorine gas, don't you agree?

Joyful turns his head away from John and remains silent John continues…
It is not an obsession nor a vendetta, it is a mission that must be continued till its accomplishment…

John makes a short pause and continues,
We owe the dead and those who are still threatened by its usage.

Joyful
How about I start Andreas Benedict's interrogations.

John

Yes, I find it to be more effective since he's familiar with my methods.

Scene 37

At the foreign office building
In the Interrogation room
Major Joyful is sitting opposite Andreas Benedict, Andreas starts a conversation,

Andreas

What is it you want to know? I can tell you anything. Perch is dead and took the secret with him.

Joyful remains silent.

Andreas

Maybe Barr should be sitting here instead of you.

Joyful

Why don't you start afresh? Just tell me all know and have had heard before Perch's death.

Andreas stands up, starts to walk around, and says,
Alles ist falsch gelaufen!
(Everything has gone wrong!)

Joyful

I am sorry, I don't speak German. What did you say?

Andreas

Forget it.

Joyful

No, help me to understand you. I would like to know what brought John and you to England.

Andreas

What do I get in return by telling you what you want to know?

Joyful

What are you thinking of?

Andreas

What do you offer?

Joyful

If we could see clearly with one eye.

Andreas with a strong and rather cold voice asks,
And then, what?

Joyful

And then, halting further production.

Andreas

Gas production, all you people say is Production! Production! How do you want to know, if it wasn't produced by you British before the Germans?

Joyful
Even then you could help us.

Andreas
How?

Joyful
It is simple, the two scientists although different in nationality, produce more or less the same type of chemical and poisonous gas.

Andreas
But with different ideologies.

Joyful
Yes, but to save one is to save the other, and to save them both, is to save the lives of yours, mine, and the rest of the human beings, wouldn't you agree?

Andreas
What you are saying, is not what you are thinking of, is it?
Joyful remains silent. Andreas looks at him and says,
Maybe but we can find something in common.
You as well as I want an end to these miseries.

Joyful
I shall help you if you could overcome your inhibitions.

Andreas
I assure you I am not the one whom you are looking for.

Joyful
I believe you.

Andreas
Do you really?

Joyful
Yes.

Andreas seems to get more and more irritated by Simon's friendliness, says,
How come you are so forthcoming?

Joyful
I don't find out the truth by using force, one tells what one wants to hear.

Andreas
You seem to be an understanding type.

Joyful
This might be but don't underestimate me.
Why did those people of yours burst into Barr's flat?

Andreas
I cannot tell why other people do or do not do what they do.

Joyful
How much do you know about the chlorine gas production laboratories, people who work there, and who are really in charge of it?

Andreas
I cannot help you. I just do not know.

Joyful
How did you get involved in this?

Andreas
Why don't you give it a name?

Joyful
How would you call it?

Andreas
Suffering.

Joyful
I find it the right definition.
Yes, indeed.

Joyful stands up and leaves the room.
Andreas remains seated and watches Joyful's steps.

Scene 38
John's Office
Joyful and John are sitting opposite one another, Joyful starts to report,
He insists on not being the scientist whom we are looking for.

John
I think what both Perch and Benedict connect, is the fact that they have been intentionally poorly informed.

Joyful
Do you mean they were used as decoys to disorientate us?

John
Yes.

Joyful
What now?

John remains silent for a short while and says,
Benedict must go back to Germany and take Perch's body with him to be buried there.

Joyful
How are we to explain this?

John
Mr Andreas Benedict will have to explain that to his superiors.

Joyful
I understand…

He doesn't continue and keeps silent whilst he is still looking at John.
John smiles.

Scene 39
Interrogation Room
Joyful enters the room with a file in his right hand whilst Benedict is sitting at the table.

He sits down opposite of Benedict, puts the file on the table, opens it, smiles, and says,
You remember, don't you? I mean as Perch was about to reveal the name…
…You know the name of the scientist who processed and produced the chlorine gas.

Benedict
What difference does that make now? You would rather want to know that he has an accomplice even here in England.

Joyful
That is interesting, tell me the name of the scientist, his accomplices and where I can find all of them.

Benedict
What will happen to me, if I tell you his name? I can tell you so much though, he is a chemist.

Joyful
Sorry, 'the Chemist', I'm sure we can think of some arrangements to help you survive.

Benedict
Surviving? Where?

Joyful
In Germany for example. You may even be able to take back Perch's body to have him buried there, in his homeland.

Benedict

Hey, stop, take it easy, as soon as I get back with or without the body, I will be accused of collaborating with you, the British.

Joyful

We might be able to help you with getting your reputation back.

Benedict

How?

Joyful

We make your scape a spectacular one and give you some secret information to take with you.

Benedict

They wouldn't be genuine, would they?

Joyful

That depends on how you sell them to your superiors, of course.
You see, we don't have use for you here as you will find out…
Who is this chemist? What is his name?

Benedict

I might tell you, his name is Fred Hub.

Joyful

You might, it is not the complete name, is it?

Benedict
It is.

Joyful
Do you assume that he might have accomplices here in England?

Benedict
That is for you to find out. But so much I can tell you that he could have himself promoted by offering his accidental discovery, as he puts it, to allow the military to use the chlorine gas as a mass-murder weapon.

Joyful nods positively and says,
I see what I can do for you and your safety.

Scene 40
Barr's Office

John
Well done, Simon.
Now we must find out if there is, indeed, a connection to us British.

Joyful
We keep Benedict here, he might be more useful than sending him back to Germany and he might even be able to identify them.

John
Do you think that he has been in contact with them?

Joyful

How else could he suggest that they are here or that they exist at all?

On the other hand, he may want to lead us to more false hints.

John

Yes, 'confusing', doesn't seem exclusive to be our business, does it?

Joyful

Yes! Where do we begin?

John looks at him and smiles.

Scene 41

General Slyer's Office

Slyer, John, and Joyful are sitting at a round table, after a short while Slyer starts a conversation, he looks at John and asks,

Any progress with your investigations?

John

Sir, I am not convinced that Benedict has had any operational activities related to the production of the gas itself.

He and the dead Perch seem to have been part of a seductive plan to irritate us.

John remains waiting for Slyer's reaction. Slyer after some seconds says,

And?

John

However, he is telling us that there might be possible conspiracies within the British.

Slyer

Within members of the army or of the civil servants?

Joyful

He leaves it to us to find it out. He mentioned the name, 'Fred Hub', though.

Slyer

Yes, an odd name was mentioned previously.
Is it now the whole name of this 'Chemist'?

John

We simply cannot decode it as if it is to be an abbreviation or as to be the full name.
We'd rather open two fronts.

Slyer

Yes, I agree.
I'll start my investigations here in England and you two form a plan for going to Germany to continue pursuit there.

John

With due respect, sir, we have been identified by the 'Deutsche Abwehr' (German Counter Espionage) and it would be a failed mission from the very beginning.

Slyer

Yes, you are right. Then we must think of a new plan.
I prioritise the finding of the scientist, the chemist of course.

John and Joyful look at one another silently as Slyer continues,
Now, Major Barr, you will work out a way for going to Germany despite the obstacles which you stressed. Dismiss!

John looks at Joyful who is still sitting and at the General and says,
Sir.

John leaves the office. Joyful remains sitting as John leaves the general's office. After John has left the office, Joyful starts a conversation,
It is getting more and more complicated, and I do not see an end to it.

General interrupts Joyful and says,
I agree with you.

Joyful
We could put an end to it.

General
Could we? And what about major Barr, could he, too?

Joyful does not answer.

General
I wouldn't blame him if he couldn't.

Both remain silent.

Scene 42
Night of the same day, outside the foreign intelligence service, Joyful comes out of the building, turns to the left, and walks away from the building block.

Scene 43
He reaches a narrow alley, turns to the right, goes into it, and continues walking. He doesn't realise that he is being shadowed by John.

Scene 44
On a foggy night, in the alley, John keeps a distance from Joyful. After a while Joyful reaches a house, rings the bell, the door opens, and he walks into the house. John walks slowly toward that house, remains standing at a distance to the house.
After an hour and a half, the door opens, and Joyful comes out of the house.
John steps forward and walks, as Joyful hears some steps which are coming from behind, stops, turns around, and sees John.

John comes closer to Joyful and says,
Good evening, Simon.

Joyful

It is you, John, good evening. What a coincidence.

John

I am afraid, it is not one.
I was tailing you.

Joyful

Why?

John

I suspected the general and you of keeping some secrets from me and the general's insistence of mission to Germany seems to put me off of this dossier.
By doing so I think now is that the chemist must have had connections here which is Benedict's assumption, too, and either one of you might be that connection.

Joyful

It is an unintentional product of a chemist by the name of, 'Fred Hub', a German national.

John

How did you find out?

Joyful

After Browning's death, the general was informed through some other channels that 'Fred' indeed, was having contacts here.

John

How come you know about these?

Joyful

I happened to get access to some reports, I fear it is more complicated than we might imagine.

John looks at him and after some seconds he turns around his head away from Joyful.

John

Whose reports?

Joyful looks at him and smiles.

Scene 45

At the same time, somewhere near the Putney Bridge, Slyer is sitting on a bench next to Man 3.
From afar, they seem to have a conversation,
After a while, they stop their conversation.
Man 3 stands up and take some steps in front of the bench, sits again as Slyer says,
I can't.

Man 3

Then I will take care of them…

Slyer

We must find an alternative to further bloodshed.

Man 3 looks at Slyer and says,

Then, find one!

Slyer remains silent. The man stands up and leaves him. From an unnoticeable distance far from Slyer, John and Joyful have been observing Slyer.

John
Have been you spying on the spy chief?

Joyful looks at John and nods positively,
I have been instructed by the newly set intelligence committee which would be the future military intelligence which will be formed into numerical divisions such as 'MI1' and 'MI2', and so on to keep watch over the daily secrecy business and keep it clean…
Its members remain anonymous, of course!

John looks at him and smiles and says and asks,
Clean, it's the most irritating definition of secrecy business.
Why are you introducing your second identity to me?

Joyful
You have proven trustworthy.

John
And the General?

Joyful
Left on his own devices, he shall be.

John
And his wife, Deborah, our colleague?

Joyful
What about her?

John
I saw her once with a man. As he realised me, he started to speak to her.

Joyful
Could you hear what he was talking?

John
No, I was not near enough but it wasn't in English.

Joyful
You saw most probably a German double agent known to us as, 'Man 1'.

John
How many men are there?

Joyful
I don't know but we can count them as soon as they try to penetrate our network.

Scene 46
The next day, at General Slyer's house. He is sitting at his desk in his study, phone rings, Slyer picks up the receiver and answers,

Slyer

Scene 47
At the same time, outside Slyer's house in a telephone booth near to his house, Joyful is holding the receiver and doesn't speak.

Scene 48
At Slyer's House.
Who's speaking, please?

Scene 49
Joyful hangs up the receiver, gets out of the telephone booth where John is standing next. They walk to Slyer's house and stand at the Slyer's house door, John rings the bell.

Scene 50
Inside the Slyer's house.
Sitting room.
They are sitting in the living room. Slyer looks at the second telephone on the table next to the door of the sitting room, turns his head back to John and Joyful, and asks,
Something to drink?

John
Yes, please.

Slyer
Sherry?

John nods positively.

Slyer
And you, Joyful?

Joyful
Yes, please.

Slyer stands up, provides them with the drinks, and continues the conversation,
What brings you here on a Sunday afternoon?

Joyful
Some…

John interrupts him by saying,
We wondered if there were some more information that you might be withholding.

Slyer
Withholding? Why would I?

Joyful
Probably we are not classified enough to know them.

Slyer
It is absurd, if there had been any additional information, you would have had knowledge of them.
I would've shared it with you.
By the way, have you finished your preparations for the mission to Germany?

John
No, sir, with due respect, sir! We do not think that it will be necessary.

Slyer
Explain!

John
All we have to look for seem to be here in England.

He looks at Joyful and Joyful says,
Yes, sir, I quite agree with major Barr.

Slyer looks at them, after some moments he smiles and says,
You would better go now. we will discuss this in the office tomorrow!

They leave the room and close the door. Sometime later, he hears knocks on the house door. He opens the door, Deborah steps in, hugs him tenderly. Slyer pushes her away from himself. Deborah pushes herself back to him. Slyer doesn't move and stands motionless in Deborah's arms as she leans her head on his shoulder. They walk into the sitting room and sit on the couch next to one another. Deborah gets closer to him, Slyer holds her tight in his arms and they start to unclothe one another. They fall on the floor in front of the coach and start making love.
…Afterwards
They are still lying on the floor in front of the coach…
The telephone rings, Slyer stands up and picks up the receiver and he hears,

Tomorrow, Chelsea flat at twenty hundred.

He puts the receiver down and goes into the kitchen which is in front of him.

Scene 51
In the kitchen
He takes a larger box out of a drawer in the kitchen shelf, empties it, takes a stick of dynamite out of the other shelf.
Deborah enters the kitchen and looks at him.
He hears a sound on the kitchen window and observes a shadow that disappears quickly.
He looks to Deborah and both of them look towards the window and again at one another.
He opens another kitchen's shelf and holds its door open for some seconds, takes a smaller box of chocolates out of it, and closes it.
He leaves the kitchen followed by Deborah.

Scene 52
They enter the living room and sit at the table.
He opens the box whilst holding the dynamite.

Scene 53
Next evening at the Chelsea Flat, Slyer is sitting at the round table. The box is wrapped in colourful wrapping paper and rounded with a ribbon and a thin cord in which one end of it goes into the box itself, the other end is outside the box and underneath the ribbon. Slyer starts to pull it very slowly.

Man 2
What do you think? Have you decided to help us?

Slyer is silent.

Man 3 says,
Now, Slyer!

Everybody who is sitting at the table looks at Slyer awaiting a response. Slyer looks at Deborah and says,
I need some more time.

Man 1 who was standing with others, takes one step back, waits and distances himself from the rest, goes near to the flat's door, opens the door, and runs out of the flat.
Deborah notices and follows him out of the Flat without being noticed.

Scene 54
At the stairway
Man 1 is running down the stairs followed by Deborah at a distance.

Scene 55
Inside the Flat
Slyer pulls on the thin cord which is underneath the ribbon with which he had wrapped the box and opens it.
Everybody is surprised.

Scene 56
Outside the building, after some seconds, Man 1 rush out of the building and pass by John and Joyful who have been observing the building? They notice that a man (Man 1) is rushing out of the building and Deborah is tailing him. John looks at Joyful...
The man turns into an alley.

Scene 57
In the ally, Man 1 who is not running any longer and is walking without haste, stops to see if he is being tailed and sees that Deborah is behind him at a distance not far from where he is standing.

Man 1
You couldn't persuade him after all.

Deborah
You were outside, looking into the kitchen through the window, weren't you?

Man 1 is looking at her.

Deborah
Didn't you want to see what General really put in that box?

Man 1
A chemistry construction box?

Deborah
You shouldn't believe what you see.

You are 'the chemist', aren't you?

Man 1
Will we ever know?

He puts his hand into his jacket's side pocket.

Deborah
If we trust one another.

Man 1 is about to pull out his hand out of his jacket pocket…

Scene 58
John who is now in the alley behind Deborah at a distance, shouts out loud,
Halt!

Scene 59
Deborah looks in the direction of the coming shout and sees John. She looks back at Man 1…

Scene 60
…who has now drawn his pistol out of his jacket's pocket,

Scene 61
Deborah drops herself on the ground…

Scene 62
…as Man 1 pulls the trigger and fires a shot.

Scene 63
John who holds his pistol with both hands fires two shots,

Scene 64
Man 1 is a deadly hit and falls on the ground.

Scene 65
John has been wounded in his right leg.
Deborah stands up and helps John standing up as Joyful joins them.
They go to Man 1 who is lying on the ground. They remain standing.

Scene 66
At the same time, Chelsea Flat. The box is now unwrapped and open with some chocolate pralines left in it. The rest of the people are still in the flat and are eating and drinking. Slyer is by the window and is looking to the street below as he hears Man 2 saying,
Der man der wegläufte!
(The man who ran away!)

Slyer
Was he the chemist?

Man 3
I can't tell, but he would have died of his poor health without going…

Slyer
You mean the chemist or the one who ran away.

Man 3
Both.

Slyer
Are helping or are you confusing me?

Man 3 remains silent.
Slyer after some seconds continues,
Yes, and he went…
…We must capture the poisonous breather and rescue the other one who inhales it.

Man 3
Whilst the poison spreads continually.

Slyer
In an endless mission.

Man 3
But there is an end to everything.

Slyer
What are you pointing out?

Man 3
You could put an end to it.

Slyer
Could I? Perhaps you tell me, 'how?'

Man 3

Let's stop these dualisms and work together.

Slyer

And you distance yourself from trading confusion?

Man 3

Confusion keeps us alive and forces us to look for a way to the truth.

Slyer

I don't agree but I understand what you are trying to establish between us.
I close this file. It seems to be the right decision…for the present that is.

Man 3

I shall follow suit.

Scene 67

Next morning at Slyer's office.
Deborah, John, and Simon are in Slyer's office and sitting around the conference table, looking at Slyer and waiting for him to start.

Slyer

The chemist is ill, on his way to an unknown and neutral country.

He looks at all of them and continues,
I am closing 'the Chemist Case!'

Deborah

And what about the consequences?

Simon

Since we now know all about it, we are beyond it and will have to live with it.

John

I remember Perch spoke the same words…
I don't want an open case.

Slyer

Neither do I…

He wraps the bundle of the file, 'The Chemist', which is in front of him, with a red stripe, stands up and puts it on a shelf behind his desk which is labelled 'Archive' and he continues, saying,
But for it to become a remembrance.

Simon and Deborah look at one another, remain silent and John looks at the shelf...

The End